Autumn's Promise

Finding Forever in Our Small Town

Clara Bridges

LPS Publishing House LLC

©Copyright 2025 - All rights reserved.

The content contained within this book may not be reproduced, duplicated, or transmitted without direct written permission from the author or the publisher.

Under no circumstances will any blame or legal responsibility be held against the publisher, or author, for any damages, reparation, or monetary loss due to the information contained within this book. Either directly or indirectly.

Legal Notice:

This book is copyright protected. This book is only for personal use. You cannot amend, distribute, sell, use, quote, or paraphrase any part, or the content within this book, without the consent of the author or publisher.

Disclaimer Notice:

Please note the information contained within this document is for educational and entertainment purposes only. All effort has been executed to present accurate, up-to-date, and reliable, complete information. No warranties of any kind are declared or implied. Readers acknowledge that the author is not engaging in the rendering of legal, financial, medical, or professional advice. The content within this book has been derived from various sources. Please consult a licensed professional before attempting any techniques outlined in this book.

By reading this document, the reader agrees that under no circumstances is the author responsible for any losses, direct or indirect, which are incurred as a result of the use of the information contained within this document, including, but not limited to, — errors, omissions, or inaccuracies.

Contents

Chapter 1
Change in the Air

The crisp scent of autumn lingers in the air, weaving through the newly restored town square. The string lights overhead cast a warm golden glow against the cobblestone paths, flickering like fireflies in the soft October breeze. The town is alive tonight—laughter spilling from the café, the hum of easy conversation drifting through the gathering crowd.

It should feel like a celebration.

It should feel safe.

But the second I see the man standing at the edge of the square, every ounce of warmth drains from my body.

He doesn't belong here.

His presence is a jagged edge against the soft serenity of Willow Creek, a shadow against the lantern light. He stands with a kind of confidence that feels out of place—too sure of himself, too at ease, as if he already knows how this night is going to end.

My stomach tightens as his gaze locks onto mine. His lips curve not quite a smile, more like an assessment, a slow unraveling of understanding.

He knows who I am.

And I have no idea who he is.

But Beau does.

Because beside me, Beau goes rigid.

His breath pulls in sharp and shallow. His hand, warm against the small of my back just moments ago, tightens slightly before falling away. Like he's instinctively withdrawing, bracing for something I don't yet understand.

I glance up at him, my pulse quickening. I've seen Beau angry before. I've seen him quiet, brooding, frustrated. But this? This is something else.

This is fear.

Not the kind that makes you run.

The kind that makes you stand your ground even when you know what's coming is bigger than you.

The man takes a step forward, his boots scraping against the cobblestone. The sound is small, barely noticeable beneath the chatter of the town, but it rings in my ears like a warning.

Then he speaks.

"Been a while."

His voice is smooth, almost amused, but there's an undercurrent of something sharper beneath it. Something calculated.

Beside me, Beau doesn't move. He doesn't breathe.

And then, just as carefully, he exhales.

"Jesse."

The name feels heavy in the air between them, thick with unspoken history.

I feel it like an entire story stretching behind us, tangled in everything Beau has never said.

Jesse's eyes flick to me, lingering, the smirk on his lips widening. "So," he muses, tilting his head slightly. "You're Daisy."

His tone makes my skin crawl. Not because it's outright threatening, but because it's *too knowing*.

Like he's already decided something about me.

I lift my chin, keeping my voice even. "And you are?"

Jesse breathes out a short, amused chuckle. "That depends on who's asking."

I don't blink. "I am."

Something flashes in his dark eyes, something sharp and entertained. "I like her," he says, flicking his gaze back to Beau. "You always did have a thing for the strong ones."

Beau moves.

It's not much just a small step forward, a shift of weight but it's enough to make Jesse's smirk falter for the briefest second.

"You don't belong here," Beau says, voice low, steady.

Jesse sighs, slipping his hands into the pockets of his worn leather jacket. "Relax, man. I just came to see an old friend. Catch up. Maybe have a drink." His gaze flicks back to me, slower this time. "Maybe make some new ones."

Beau is in front of me before I can react, blocking Jesse from view. His body is tight, his stance rigid, but his voice?

Lethal.

"Don't."

Jesse lifts his hands in mock surrender. "Touchy, touchy." His smirk returns, but this time it's more deliberate. "That's new. You never used to be so protective."

Beau doesn't answer.

But I see the way his fists clench at his sides, the way his jaw tightens, the way he's holding back something that wants to come out.

My heart hammers.

Who *is* this man?

The air between them crackles, charged with something thick and unreadable. Jesse watches Beau like he's waiting, like he *wants* him to react. Like this moment, this *reunion* is a game he's been planning for a long time.

Finally, Beau exhales sharply.

"What do you want?"

Jesse hums, tapping his fingers against the side of his jeans. "Straight to the point. Always liked that about you."

"Jesse," Beau grits out, his voice tighter now. "Why are you here?"

A beat of silence passes as Jesse's smirk fades.

And for the first time, I see it. The crack in his perfectly cool demeanor. The flash of something real beneath the surface.

He *wants* something.

And whatever it is— it is not good.

Jesse sighs, shifting his weight. "Look, I was in the area, and I thought why not stop by? See how my old friend is doing?" He pauses, studying Beau, his smirk returning like he enjoys what he sees. "You've built a nice little life here. Pretty town. Pretty girl."

I tense.

Beau *moves*.

It's small like a twitch, a fraction of an inch but Jesse catches it. And he *grins*.

"Still have that temper, huh?" Jesse muses, shaking his head. "Relax, Beau. I'm not here to start trouble. Just wanted to see you."

Beau lets out a slow breath, running a hand down his face. "You saw me. Now leave."

Jesse tilts his head, amused. "Nah. I think I'll stick around for a bit."

A sick, twisting feeling curls in my stomach.

He's *pushing*.

Testing.

Waiting to see if Beau will break.

Beau's nostrils flare, but he doesn't snap. Not yet. Instead, his voice drops lower, steadier.

"Jesse," he says quietly, "you shouldn't be here."

Something unreadable flickers across Jesse's face, just for a second. Then just as quickly—it's gone.

He exhales, rocking back on his heels. "Well," he says, "I guess we'll see about that."

Then, with one last glance in my direction one final, knowing smirk as Jesse turns and walks away.

Not far.

Not fast.

Like he *wants* us to know he's not actually leaving.

Like this is just the beginning.

Beau doesn't move until Jesse disappears around the corner.

Only then does he exhale, his whole body seeming to deflate, his shoulders sinking under an invisible weight.

I reach for his arm, my pulse still racing. "Beau—"

"Not here." His voice is quiet, urgent. He laces his fingers through mine, tugging me gently but firmly away from the town square, away from the lingering eyes of anyone who might have caught that exchange.

His grip is tight. His breath is unsteady.

And beneath it all, I feel it.

The shift.

The unraveling.

The quiet, creeping promise that whatever peace we thought we had found?

It was never real.

Because the past?

It always, always comes back.

Chapter 2
The Weight of the Past

The night air presses against my skin, thick with the scent of damp leaves and burning wood from a distant bonfire. The town square hums with life from the music spilling from the café to bursts of laughter from families still gathered beneath the lanterns but it all feels wrong.

Like the world is still spinning, but I've somehow stepped outside of it.

Because Beau's face is pale.

His jaw is tight.

And his words are still hanging between us, heavier than the autumn air.

"A mistake I thought I left behind."

I swallow, my pulse pounding against my ribs as I take a slow step closer to him. His shoulders are still tense, like he's bracing for impact, for me to demand answers.

And maybe I should.

Maybe I should push him, make him tell me who Jesse is, what he wants, why he's here now after all this time.

But all I can manage is a quiet, "Beau."

His eyes flick to mine, a storm raging in their depths. His fingers flex at his sides, like he wants to reach for me but doesn't trust himself to.

Like he's afraid that if he touches me, this moment—this fragile, terrifying moment will shatter completely.

I wet my lips, my voice barely above a whisper. "Tell me."

Beau exhales sharply, dragging a hand down his face, and for a long moment, I think he might.

But then—

"No," he mutters, shaking his head, his voice rough and low. "Not here."

Not here.

Because there are people watching. Because the town is still awake, still moving, still living.

Because whatever this is—it's not meant to be heard.

A chill snakes down my spine.

Beau's secrets used to be quiet ones, the kind he buried deep, only letting them surface in slow, careful pieces.

But this?

This is something else entirely.

This isn't just hesitation.

This is fear.

And that scares me more than anything.

I glance past him, toward the spot where Jesse had stood just minutes ago.

He is gone now, but that doesn't mean anything. Because even if I cannot see him, I can still feel him lingering in the shadows, waiting for the right moment to step back into the light. Pulling at whatever thread of Beau's past he's come here to unravel.

My stomach twists, but I force myself to focus. "Okay," I say softly, nodding. "Then let's go."

Beau's brow furrows. "Go where?"

"Somewhere private. Somewhere you can actually talk to me instead of standing here acting like you're waiting for the ground to cave in."

He exhales through his nose, glancing around the square like he's just now realizing where we are. Like he forgot people were here, watching.

A group of older men near the bakery nod in our direction before returning to their conversation. A few of Maggie's regulars eye us curiously from outside the café, their chatter slowing just a bit.

Beau notices all of it.

And he hates it.

Because Beau Montgomery doesn't like being the center of attention.

And right now?

Jesse has made sure that's exactly where he is.

His jaw clenches, his hands balling into fists at his sides before he finally exhales, his voice tight.

"Let's go."

He doesn't ask where.

He doesn't say another word.

He just grabs my hand, grips it tightly, and pulls me away from the square.

Away from the lingering stares.

Away from the ghosts trying to claw their way back into the present.

And as we disappear into the night, I can't shake the feeling that whatever Beau is about to tell me—it's going to change everything.

The drive is silent.

Beau's hands are tight on the steering wheel, his knuckles pale beneath the dim dashboard light. His jaw stays locked, his breaths controlled but uneven.

I don't speak.

Not yet.

Because I know Beau.

And Beau is still fighting himself.

Still debating how much he should say, how much he should keep locked away.

I won't push. Not now.

But I will wait.

Because I refuse to let this turn into another secret that festers.

By the time he pulls off the main road and onto the dirt path leading to his cabin, my heart is pounding. The woods stretch around us, towering pines swaying in the wind, their shadows long and reaching.

The place is quiet. Still.

The kind of quiet that holds history in its silence.

I swallow hard as he parks the truck, cutting the engine.

The air inside feels too thick, too loaded.

But Beau doesn't move.

He just sits there, staring straight ahead, fingers still gripping the wheel.

For a long moment, I wonder if he's going to say anything at all.

"He was my brother's best friend."

I blink, my breath catching. "What?"

Beau finally looks at me, his eyes dark and unreadable.

"Jesse," he says, voice tight. "He was my brother's best friend."

I stare at him, my pulse hammering. "Your brother?"

Beau nods once. "Aaron."

Aaron.

I don't know much about Beau's brother. He's mentioned him a handful of times, always in passing. There was never a deep dive, never any details, just an understanding that Aaron was part of a life Beau didn't talk about.

I lean forward slightly, my voice softer now. "Beau... what happened?"

Beau exhales, raking a hand through his hair.

Then, finally, he speaks.

"Aaron and Jesse were inseparable growing up. They got into trouble together, ran with the same crowd, did things they shouldn't have. But Aaron—he was different. He wanted out."

My stomach twists. "Out of what?"

Beau's throat bobs. "The kind of life you don't just walk away from."

A chill prickles at my skin.

Beau swallows, his gaze distant. "Jesse didn't like that. And the night Aaron finally decided to leave—for good... something happened."

Something *bad*.

Something unspoken.

I inch closer, my breath barely making it past my lips. "Beau..."

He turns to me then, his eyes locked onto mine, something raw and aching in his gaze.

"Aaron didn't make it out."

The words hit like a gut punch.

I suck in a sharp breath, my chest tightening. "Beau..."

"I don't know what happened that night," he continues, his voice quieter now. "But Jesse does."

My stomach drops. "You think he—"

"I don't *think*," Beau cuts in, his voice sharp. "I *know*."

I stare at him, my pulse hammering, my mind spinning.

Jesse isn't just an old ghost from Beau's past.

He's the reason Beau lost his brother and now he's back.

I shake my head, my hands curling into fists in my lap. "Why now? Why after all this time?"

Beau's jaw tightens, his eyes flashing with something dark.

"I don't know."

Silence hangs between us, stretching, twisting, pulling at every frayed edge.

Then finally Beau exhales, dragging a hand through his hair before looking at me, his gaze softer now, but no less intense.

"I didn't want you in the middle of this," he says, his voice low. "I didn't want *us* tangled up in this."

I hold his gaze, steady and certain.

"You don't get to decide that," I whisper.

Something flickers across his face—something vulnerable.

And then, for the first time since Jesse showed up, Beau reaches for me.

Pulls me close.

And just holds on.

Like I'm the only thing keeping him from falling apart completely.

Chapter 3
An Unexpected Reunion

The weight of Beau's arms around me is heavy, grounding, but the storm inside him rages on. I can feel it in the way his muscles stay tense, his fingers gripping the back of my sweater like he's afraid to let go.

Like he thinks if he does, I'll slip through his fingers, too.

Like Aaron did.

As if he's terrified Jesse is here to take something else away from him.

The thought makes my stomach twist, but I don't pull back.

Not yet.

Outside, the wind rattles through the trees, rustling leaves against the windowpane, whispering secrets only the night can hear. The fire Beau built earlier crackles in the hearth, sending soft, flickering light across the cabin walls, but it does little to warm the coldness settling in my chest.

Jesse, Beau's past and a brother lost, A night that changed everything.

Now that Jesse is back, and no one knows why.

Beau's breath is warm against my hair, slow but uneven, like he's trying to steady himself, to hold back whatever's threatening to claw its way out.

And maybe I should let him sit with it. Maybe I should give him the space he so clearly thinks he needs.

But I can't.

Because I need answers.

And whether he's ready or not, so does he.

I pull back just enough to look up at him, my hands sliding down his arms until my fingers lace through his.

He's warm. Solid.

But his grip?

Just a little too tight.

"Beau." My voice is soft, coaxing.

He doesn't look at me.

I squeeze his hands. "Talk to me."

His jaw tenses, and for a second, I think he won't but he manages to get a few words out.

"I don't know what he wants." His voice is hoarse, raw, his eyes locked on a spot on the floor like it holds some kind of answer. "I don't know why he's here *now*, after all these years. But I do know one thing."

I swallow hard. "What?"

Beau's fingers tighten around mine, his eyes dark when they finally meet mine.

"I don't trust him."

A shiver runs through me at the way he says it is low, certain, edged with something sharp.

Something that tells me this isn't just about an old friend turned enemy.

This is about a man who's capable of more than I understand.

A man who took his brother away from him.

I inhale slowly, steadying myself. "Then we figure out why he's here. We don't let him catch you off guard."

Beau shakes his head, his fingers slipping from mine as he runs a hand down his face. "I can handle Jesse, Daisy."

Something about the way he says it is so final, so closed off making irritation flare hot in my chest.

"Alone?" I challenge myself.

His silence is my answer.

I fold my arms, my stomach twisting. "Beau, this isn't just *your* problem. It's ours now. You know that, right?"

His nostrils flare, frustration flickering across his face, but he doesn't argue.

Doesn't agree, either.

I press forward. "You're not shutting me out of this."

He lets out a slow, measured breath, but I can see the war waging inside him. The part of him that wants to pull me closer. And the part that wants to keep me far, far away.

But I already know the truth.

Jesse is here.

And he isn't going anywhere.

The smell of fresh coffee and cinnamon drifts through Willow Creek's main street, wrapping the town in a warm, familiar embrace.

If I hadn't spent last night tangled in Beau's past, I might have been able to enjoy it.

But my head is still buzzing between Jesse and Aaron and everything in-between. A night Beau won't talk about.

I let out a slow breath, pushing through the door of Maggie's café, the soft chime of the bell barely registering over the noise inside. The morning rush is in full swing—locals chatting over steaming cups, a group of teenagers crowded in the corner laughing over their phones, a couple arguing about who forgot to take the trash out.

Normal and simple, everything that night wasn't.

Maggie catches my eye from behind the counter, her brows lifting as she waves me over.

"You look like hell."

I sigh, dropping onto a stool. "Good morning to you too."

She snorts, setting a cup of coffee in front of me before leaning against the counter, arms crossed. "Alright, spill. You left the festival early with Beau last night, and now you're staring at that coffee like it holds the meaning of life."

I stare at the steam curling from the mug, debating where to even start.

And then, before I can stop myself—

"Jesse's back."

Maggie stills.

The playful spark in her eyes dims, her body going rigid.

Slowly, she lowers herself onto the stool beside me.

"Well," she says, voice carefully measured, "that's... not great."

A humorless laugh escapes me. "No. It's not."

She exhales, rubbing her temples. "Why the hell would he come back *now*?"

"That's the question of the day."

Maggie frowns, biting her lip. "Have you asked Beau?"

"Yeah," I say, swirling my spoon through the coffee. "And I got a whole lot of *I don't know* and *don't worry about it* in return."

She huffs. "Sounds like him."

"Yeah, well, I'm *not* just ignoring this." I glance at her, my jaw tightening. "You know something, don't you?"

Maggie hesitates.

I sit up straighter. "Maggie."

She exhales sharply, shaking her head. "I don't *know* anything, Daisy. But I *heard* things. Back when it all happened. Back when Beau left home for good."

My heart pounds. "What kind of things?"

Maggie looks around the café, like she's making sure no one is listening. Then, she leans in, voice dropping.

"There was talk," she murmurs. "That Aaron was trying to cut ties with *someone*. That Jesse didn't take it well."

The air turns thick.

I grip my mug tighter. "And?"

Maggie hesitates. "And the night Aaron died? Jesse disappeared."

A cold chill races down my spine, and I force myself to breathe, to think, to piece the fragments together. Jesse disappeared the night Aaron died, and now he has returned. The realization twists my stomach, and I push my coffee away, unable to swallow another sip.

"I have to talk to him," I whisper.

Maggie goes still, her eyes sharp. "To who?"

My throat tightens as I swallow hard. "Jesse."

I don't expect to find him so soon.

But as I step outside the café, heart still pounding, the morning sun glinting off the storefront windows—

He's *there*.

Leaning against the lamppost, watching me.

Like he knew I'd be here.

Like he's *been* waiting.

Jesse smirks, tipping an imaginary hat in my direction.

"Morning, Daisy."

My breath catches.

I should turn around. Walk back inside. *Think this through.*

But I don't.

I step forward.

Because whatever this game is, I'm not letting Jesse play it alone.

Chapter 4
Growing Tensions

Jesse's smirk is slow; deliberate like he's been waiting for this exact moment. Like he *knew* I'd come looking for him before I even knew it myself.

That alone makes me want to turn around and walk straight back into the café.

But I don't.

I *can't.*

Because the second I do, I lose.

I don't even know what the game is yet, but I can already feel the quiet push-and-pull, the subtle battle for control. And if there's one thing I've learned from being with Beau, it's that Jesse doesn't do anything without a reason.

So, I take a step forward. Not too close. Not too far. Just enough to show him that I am not afraid. At least, that is what I want him to believe. My pulse pounds in my throat, every nerve in my body urging me to run.

Jesse watches me carefully, tilting his head, his dark eyes sharp with amusement. "Didn't expect to see you out here all alone."

His voice is smooth, easy. A little too comfortable.

I fold my arms, lifting my chin. "Didn't expect to see *you* in Willow Creek at all."

His smirk widens. "Guess we're both full of surprises."

A muscle ticks in my jaw. I don't have time for this.

I take a slow breath. "Why are you here, Jesse?"

The corner of his mouth twitches, like he was expecting me to ask but not quite so directly. "Straight to the point. I like that."

I don't respond. I just stare at him, waiting, refusing to give him the satisfaction of a reaction. His smirk lingers, sharp and infuriating, but I catch the flicker in his eyes. It's something darker, more serious, like he's weighing a decision he hasn't quite made. The silence stretches until, finally, he speaks.

"I came to talk to Beau."

There's a weight to the way he says it, an underlying challenge.

I keep my expression steady. "You had your chance last night."

Jesse exhales slowly, running a hand through his hair. "Yeah, well. That didn't go the way I planned."

Something sharp flickers in his gaze, gone as quickly as it appeared.

I fight the urge to step back. "What *is* the plan, Jesse? Because right now, it looks an awful lot like you're just here to stir things up."

He chuckles. "That what Beau told you?"

I don't answer.

Because it *is* what Beau told me. And it's probably true.

But part of me—the part I don't want to admit exists and wants to hear Jesse's side.

Not because I trust him.

But because I need to know what we're up against.

Jesse shifts his weight, glancing toward the street where the morning crowd moves in easy rhythms with shop doors swinging open, laughter spilling from the bakery, Maggie's voice carrying from inside the café.

Then, his eyes snap back to mine.

"I just need a conversation, Daisy." His voice drops, quieter now. *Sincere.* "That's all."

My stomach twists.

Because I don't believe him, not for a second.

But there's something in his expression, some flicker of truth beneath the layers of manipulation that makes my fingers curl into fists at my sides.

Something that makes me wonder if maybe... just maybe... he actually does have unfinished business.

And not just with Beau.

I swallow hard, ignoring the way my gut is screaming at me.

"You want to talk to him?" I say, forcing my voice to stay even. "Then say what you need to say, and leave."

Jesse's smirk falters for a fraction of a second. "That simple, huh?"

"Yes."

He exhales a quiet laugh, shaking his head. "See, I don't think it is."

My pulse jumps.

He takes a step forward. Not close enough to touch, but close enough that I have to fight the instinct to move back.

"Because if it *was* that simple, Beau would've talked to me already." Jesse's voice is lower now, softer like he's letting me in on a secret. "But he hasn't. Has he?"

I clench my jaw.

Because Jesse might be playing a game—

But he's not wrong.

Beau *hasn't* talked to him.

And I don't know if it's because he's angry. Or scared. Or both.

But I do know one thing—if Jesse wants something from him, he's not leaving until he gets it.

And if I walk away now, I'm letting him control that.

Letting him control *Beau*.

And I won't let that happen, I refuse.

I straighten my shoulders. "If you want to talk to Beau, then talk."

Jesse studies me, his lips curving slightly, but his eyes are unreadable.

Then he stalks forward and in a threatening tone he asks,

"You sure you want me to do that, Daisy?"

A chill prickles at my spine.

The way he says my name is slow, deliberate and makes something inside me twist.

Like there's something he knows that I don't.

Like there's something I should be afraid of.

And that?

That's the part that scares me the most.

I swallow hard. "I'm sure."

Jesse's smirk lingers, but his gaze sharpens.

Then, with one last glance toward the café, he exhales.

"Alright, then."

And just like that I know I've set something in motion.

Something I might not be able to stop.

Beau is already pacing when I get back.

His movements are restless, his shoulders stiff, his fingers raking through his hair in quick, uneven motions.

He looks up the second I step inside, his eyes narrowing. "Where were you?"

My stomach tightens. "Beau—"

His expression darkens. "Daisy."

I hesitate for half a second.

And that's all it takes.

His voice drops, low and rough. "Tell me you didn't talk to him."

I inhale sharply. "Beau—"

"*Damn it.*"

The frustration in his voice slams into me like a physical thing.

I step forward, my pulse racing. "You don't get to shut me out of this."

Beau exhales sharply, rubbing his jaw, shaking his head like he can't believe I did it. "I told you—"

"You *told me* Jesse is dangerous." My voice rises, sharp and unrelenting. "And I *believe* you. But ignoring him? That's not gonna make him disappear."

Beau clenches his jaw. "So what, Daisy? You think talking to him will?"

I hold his gaze, steady. "I think he's not leaving until you do."

The silence between us is thick and unforgiving.

"What did he say?" Beau's voice is quieter now, but no less intense.

I exhale. "That he wants to talk to you."

Beau lets out a bitter laugh, shaking his head. "Yeah. I bet he does."

"He's not gonna stop, Beau." My voice softens, but I don't back down. "Not until he gets whatever it is he came here for."

Beau doesn't respond.

Just clenches his fists.

And I see it—the war in his eyes.

The part of him that wants to protect me.

And also, the part of him that knows I'm right.

He exhales, tilting his head back, eyes closed for a long moment.

"When?" is all, he manages to get out.

I blink, caught off guard. "What?"

Beau's jaw tightens as he looks at me. "When does he want to talk?"

A slow breath slips past my lips as the realization settles deep inside me. This is it. The moment Beau has been trying to outrun, the moment he's kept buried for so long. His past has finally caught up to him, and now there's no way to escape it.

Chapter 5

Growing Tensions

D on't move.

Every instinct in me screams to turn around, to walk back inside the café where Maggie is, where warmth and safety exist, where Jesse *isn't*.

But I don't.

I stand there, the cool autumn air biting at my skin, my hands curling into fists at my sides.

Jesse leans against the lamppost like he has all the time in the world, like this meeting isn't a *big deal*—like he didn't just tear open a wound that Beau's spent years trying to stitch closed.

He's waiting.

For what, I don't know.

For me to say something? To turn and run? To acknowledge the unspoken truth hanging between us?

I swallow, steadying myself before taking a slow, deliberate step forward.

This might be a mistake.

But *not knowing* is worse.

I lift my chin. "You've been waiting for me."

Jesse's mouth twitches, something amused flickering across his face. "Maybe."

I narrow my eyes. "Why?"

He lets out a quiet hum, tilting his head as if considering. "You ask a lot of questions."

"You show up out of nowhere and expect me *not* to?"

His smirk deepens, but it doesn't reach his eyes. "Fair enough."

I don't move. I don't breathe too hard. I just watch him, trying to piece him together—this stranger who *knows too much* and *says too little.*

His jacket is worn, but expensive. His boots are scuffed but solid. His posture is loose, lazy, but there's an edge underneath it like a coiled wire, waiting to snap.

He is a contradiction, a man who doesn't belong in a town like this, someone who feels carved from another world entirely. And yet, despite everything that doesn't fit, everything that shouldn't make sense but here he is, standing in front of me like he was always meant to be "Why are you here, Jesse?" I ask again, voice quieter this time.

Jesse lets out a slow breath, glancing past me toward the café window, where Maggie is probably *watching this exact conversation.*

Then his gaze flicks back to mine.

"Beau didn't tell you?"

I hate how my stomach twists at that.

Because *no, he didn't.*

Not really.

Not enough.

"He told me you were Aaron's friend."

Jesse's expression shifts, just slightly. It's there and gone in a flash, but I *see* it. A flicker of something behind his eyes—something dark, something haunted.

Then, just as quickly, it's buried again.

"And?" Jesse prompts.

I hold my ground. "And that he doesn't trust you."

A beat of silence.

Jesse laughs it's low, amused and cold.

"Yeah," he says, shaking his head, rubbing his jaw like he's heard this before. "That sounds about right."

I swallow, my pulse hammering. "So why come back?"

Jesse exhales, pushing off the lamppost, stepping closer—*not too close, but close enough* that I feel the shift in energy between us.

"I'll tell you something, Daisy." His voice is softer now, but not gentle. "When someone leaves behind unfinished business, it has a way of following them. No matter how far they try to run."

Something *icy* curls around my spine.

"Are you talking about Aaron?" I ask, barely above a whisper.

Jesse's expression stills.

His jaw ticks.

For a second, I swear I see something crack in him, something real, something raw—

But then it's gone.

His face smooths, his shoulders rolling back as he lets out a slow, easy breath. "You ask a lot of questions, Daisy."

I clench my jaw. "You already said that."

He grins. "Guess I did."

I take a step back. I don't trust him. I don't trust a damn thing about him. But I *know* he came here for a reason.

And I also know, He's not going to tell me what it is, not yet.

"You want something from Beau," I say, testing the waters. "Don't you?"

Jesse's grin fades, just slightly.

"You're sharp," he murmurs.

I fold my arms. "Beau doesn't owe you anything."

Something flickers in his expression—something unreadable.

Then, he exhales, shaking his head. "That's where you're wrong."

I don't get the chance to respond.

Because just then a voice cuts through the air.

"Daisy."

I whip around.

Beau is standing just feet away, his body tense, his eyes locked on Jesse like he's looking at something out of a nightmare.

Jesse smirks, rocking back on his heels. "Well, speak of the devil."

Beau moves before I can stop him.

He crosses the distance fast, his hand catching my wrist, pulling me back, behind him.

Not gently.

Not casually.

But like it's instinct.

Jesse watches, brows lifting slightly. "Easy, man."

Beau doesn't speak. Doesn't blink. He just stares.

His body is stiff, his breathing controlled but shallow.

I glance up at him, my pulse hammering. "Beau—"

"Get inside, Daisy," Beau says, his voice quiet, rough.

I hesitate.

"Now."

I swallow hard.

I don't want to leave him.

I don't want to back down.

But there's something in his voice, it's something final, something dangerous that makes my stomach drop.

Jesse notices too.

His smirk twitches. "Look at that," he muses. "You *have* changed."

Beau's jaw tightens. "I told you to leave."

Jesse doesn't move.

He just watches him. Studying. Calculating.

"I'm not here for trouble," Jesse says, and for the first time, I *almost* believe him.

Beau exhales sharply, shaking his head. "Yeah? Then what the hell do you want?"

Jesse's eyes flicker. "Just to talk."

Beau laughs—but there's nothing amused about it.

"You lost that right a long time ago."

A heavy pause.

And then, Jesse's voice drops.

"Did I?"

The weight of those two words hits **hard**.

Beau stills.

And for the first time, I see it— the hesitation, almost doubt.

Because maybe Beau *knows* something I don't.

Maybe Jesse *does* have unfinished business.

And maybe...

Just maybe—

It's something Beau *never* wanted to face.

I don't want to leave.

I don't want to walk away from this, from Beau, from the truth that's hovering just out of reach.

But I also know this isn't my fight.

Not yet.

Not until Beau lets me in.

And right now?

He's not there yet.

So, I make a choice.

I step back.

And as I turn toward the café, Jesse speaks one last time.

"You can only bury the past for so long, Montgomery."

Beau doesn't answer.

And as I slip inside, heart pounding, I know that we are about to learn the real reason why Jesse has sought Beau out.

Chapter 6
Up in the Air

I don't go far.

I tell myself I will. That I'll listen to Beau. That I'll give him space. That I'll let him deal with Jesse the way *he* needs to.

But my feet refuse to move farther than the doorway of Maggie's café.

I stand just inside, the scent of fresh coffee and baked cinnamon rolls swirling around me, but my stomach is too tight, my breath too unsteady to feel any kind of comfort.

Through the window, I can still see them.

Beau. Jesse.

Two men standing inches apart, carrying the weight of something old, something broken, something dangerous between them.

Their words are muffled by the glass, but their body language says everything.

Beau is rigid. Stiff. His hands clenched into tight fists at his sides, his chest rising and falling in slow, measured breaths—the kind he takes when he's holding back.

And Jesse?

Jesse is the opposite. Loose. Relaxed. His head tilted, that same unreadable smirk on his face like he's *waiting* for something.

Waiting for Beau to snap.

Waiting for control to slip.

I bite my lip, my pulse hammering.

Beau is so careful with his anger. He keeps it locked away, buried beneath layers of silence and restraint. But I've seen it before.

I've seen what happens when he reaches his limit.

And Jesse?

Jesse looks like someone who *wants* to find out exactly what that limit is.

I clench my fists, nails pressing into my palms.

Go inside, Daisy. Let him handle this.

But what if he *can't*?

What if this is the one fight he isn't ready for?

A warm hand lands on my arm, startling me.

I whirl around to find Maggie watching me, her eyes dark with concern.

"You're staring," she says, her voice low.

I exhale sharply. "I know."

Maggie's gaze flickers toward the window, then back to me. "You need to let him handle it."

"I *am*," I say, too quickly.

Maggie arches a brow. "Uh-huh. That's why you're standing here looking like you're about to run out there and throw yourself in the middle of it?"

I swallow hard, my chest tightening.

Because the truth is—I *want* to.

I want to walk right back out there, grab Beau's hand, pull him away from whatever this is before it spirals into something neither of us can undo.

But I can't.

Not yet.

Not until I *understand*.

"Why does it feel like Jesse's in control of this?" I ask, my voice barely above a whisper.

Maggie exhales, rubbing the back of her neck. "Because he *wants* to be. That's what guys like him do, Daisy. They show up, act like they know more than they do, get inside people's heads."

I shake my head. "No. This is different."

Maggie studies me carefully. "Different how?"

I hesitate.

Because I don't know *how* to explain it.

How to explain the weight in Jesse's voice. The way he spoke to Beau like he was owed something.

The way Beau looked at him—not just with anger, but with guilt.

A deep, buried guilt I've *never* seen in him before.

"I think," I murmur, voice tight, "Jesse knows something about Aaron's death that Beau doesn't."

Maggie stills.

She doesn't argue.

She doesn't try to dismiss it.

Because we both know it's possible.

Because Jesse disappeared the night Aaron died.

And now he's back.

And Beau—

Beau is unraveling.

I risk another glance outside.

Beau's face is tight; his shoulders coiled with tension. Jesse is speaking, his expression unreadable. But then—

Beau flinches.

Just barely.

Just enough for me to *see it*.

I suck in a sharp breath.

Because whatever Jesse just said—

It hit its mark.

And Beau is *breaking*.

I don't realize I'm moving until Maggie catches my wrist.

"Daisy," she warns.

I shake my head, my chest aching. "I can't—"

"You *have* to."

I snap my gaze to hers, my pulse racing.

Maggie's face softens, just slightly. "Daisy. He needs to come to *you* when he's ready. Not because you forced it. Not because you ran after him the second he looked like he might fall apart. But because he *chose* to let you in."

I swallow hard, my throat thick. "And what if he never does?"

Maggie doesn't answer.

Because we *both* know the risk.

But I also know one thing—

If Beau doesn't let me in, Jesse *will*.

And I don't know which truth scares me more.

Beau doesn't come to me.

Not right away.

Not until hours later, when the sun has long since disappeared and the night air carries the scent of damp pine and burning firewood.

I hear his truck before I see him.

The crunch of tires on gravel. The soft hum of the engine before it cuts off.

I don't move from where I'm sitting on the porch swing.

I just *wait*.

Seconds pass. Then minutes.

Finally, I hear footsteps but they are slow, hesitant.

I grip the blanket wrapped around my shoulders tighter, my heart pounding as Beau steps into view.

His face is unreadable, his hair a mess like he's been running his hands through it all night. His flannel is wrinkled; his jeans dusted with dirt.

He looks tired and worn out like he's been carrying too much for far too long.

I inhale slowly, watching as he stops at the edge of the porch steps, his hands shoved deep in his pockets.

For a long moment, neither of us speaks.

"I shouldn't have let you talk to him."

His voice is rough.

I shake my head. "You didn't let me. I *chose* to."

His jaw clenches. "You don't know him, Daisy. You don't—"

"Neither do *you*," I cut in.

Beau's eyes flash. "I know enough."

I hold his gaze, steady and sure. "Then *tell me*."

But I'm met with silence.

Beau exhales sharply, dragging a hand through his hair before stepping onto the porch.

He doesn't sit beside me.

He paces.

Like he's trying to burn off the restless energy in his veins.

Like he's trying to decide what to tell me.

I watch him, my heart aching.

"Beau." My voice is softer now. "I *want* to help you. But I can't if you don't—"

"He thinks I owe him," Beau murmurs, cutting me off.

I still. "What?"

Beau stops pacing, turning toward me. His eyes are darker now, filled with something I can't name.

"He thinks I owe him," he repeats, voice rough. "For what happened to Aaron."

A sharp breath leaves my lips. "Beau—"

"He thinks it's my fault," Beau mutters, his jaw tight. "And maybe—" He stops himself, shaking his head.

I sit up straighter. "*Maybe what?*"

His throat bobs.

"Maybe he's right."

The words gut me.

Because they *shouldn't* be true.

But Beau—

Beau believes they are.

And for the first time, I realize—

This fight with Jesse?

This *isn't* about the past.

It's about Beau's guilt.

And I don't know how to pull him out of it.

Chapter 7
The Confession

Maybe he's right.

The words are still hanging in the air, thick and suffocating, wrapping around my ribs and squeezing.

I *stare* at Beau.

At the man I love. The man who has always been steady, solid—even when he's been quiet, even when he's carried too much, even when he's kept parts of himself locked away.

But right now?

Right now, I don't recognize the look in his eyes.

The weight of his guilt.

The kind of self-blame that doesn't just sit on your shoulders, it sinks into your bones.

I wet my lips, my pulse hammering. "Beau—"

He shakes his head, exhaling sharply as he takes a step back, like he already regrets saying it. Like he wants to take it back.

But I won't let him.

I push off the porch swing, dropping the blanket that was wrapped around my shoulders. The night air bites at my skin, but I don't care.

I step toward him.

"Don't do that," I say, my voice quieter now, softer. "Don't say something like that and then shut down."

Beau's jaw flexes. His hands ball into fists at his sides.

"I'm not shutting down."

I arch a brow. "No? Then tell me what you meant."

His throat bobs. His gaze flicks away. "It's not—" He stops, dragging a rough hand down his face before inhaling sharply. "It doesn't matter."

I *snap.*

"It *does* matter." My voice rises before I can stop it, frustration and worry twisting together. "You *matter*, Beau. And if you think for one second, I'm just going to let you stand there and—"

"I could have stopped it."

The words crash into me like a wrecking ball.

I freeze.

Beau's chest rises and falls in slow, heavy breaths. His eyes stay locked on me, dark and raw and full of something aching.

"I could have stopped it," he repeats, his voice rough, hollow. "Aaron is leaving. Jesse getting to him first. The whole darn thing."

I swallow, my mouth suddenly dry. "Beau... what are you talking about?"

A beat of silence.

Then—

He *breaks*.

"I should have been with him that night."

The words spill out of him like they've been held back for years, like once they start, they won't stop.

Like he's drowning in them.

I barely breathe. I just *listen*.

"We fought." Beau's voice is quiet, like he's talking to himself more than me. "Aaron wanted out—out of all of it. Jesse, the people he ran with, the mistakes he made. He was ready."

His jaw tightens, his hands gripping the porch railing now, his knuckles white.

"But I told him it was too late. That Jesse wouldn't let him just walk away. That he had to be *smart* about it. That he had to wait."

A sharp breath leaves my lips. "Beau—"

"I thought I was *protecting* him." His voice cracks. "I thought if I could just *get through to him*, if I could just *make him see reason*, he'd stay put. He wouldn't do something reckless. He wouldn't—"

He stops. Swallows.

When he looks at me again, I feel my heart *shatter*.

Because I see it now.

I see the moment Beau Montgomery started blaming himself for something that was never his fault.

"Aaron didn't listen." His throat bobs. "He went to Jesse that night anyway. Told him he was done. That he was leaving. That he was never coming back."

I shake my head, my breath shallow. "Beau, none of that—"

"He never made it home."

My stomach *drops*.

The finality in his voice, the grief woven into every syllable—is enough to steal the air from my lungs.

I stare at him, my pulse hammering.

And for the first time, I see it.

The guilt that has been eating him alive for years.

He thinks it's *his* fault.

That if he had gone with Aaron. If he had fought harder. If he had stopped him.

Maybe his brother would still be here.

Tears sting my eyes. "Beau."

He exhales, raking a hand through his hair before finally—*finally* meeting my gaze again.

"There's something else," he murmurs.

I brace myself.

"Jesse was the last person to see Aaron alive."

The words send a chill racing down my spine.

"I know," I whisper.

Beau's eyes darken. "Then you know why I can't trust him."

I nod. "Yes. But do *you* know why he's back?"

Silence.

Beau's gaze flickers, uncertainty slipping through the cracks of his frustration. "No."

I step closer. "Then don't let him be the one who controls this."

Beau exhales sharply. "You think I'm *letting* him control this?"

I shake my head. "Not intentionally. But Beau, if Jesse *does* know something about that night... don't you want to know the truth?"

A muscle feathers in his jaw.

"I already know the truth."

I arch a brow. "Do you?"

A beat of silence.

Something shifts in his expression.

Doubt.

For the first time, real doubt.

Because maybe—just *maybe*—he's spent so long believing *his version* of that night, he's never let himself ask:

What if I was wrong?

Beau rubs a hand over his face before exhaling hard. "I don't know, Daisy."

I reach for his hand, gripping it tightly. "Then let's find out. *Together.*"

His fingers tighten around mine, his pulse strong beneath my touch.

But he doesn't answer right away.

Instead, he studies me.

Like he's weighing something.

Like he's trying to decide if letting me be part of this assessing if *pulling me in* is worth the risk.

I already know what he's thinking.

He's afraid.

Not just for himself.

But for *me*, for us.

And maybe if this were months ago, maybe if we were still figuring out what we meant to each other, maybe if I weren't already so *in this*, I'd let him pull away.

But I won't.

Because I love him.

And loving someone means standing beside them—even when they don't know if they can stand at all.

So, I squeeze his hand.

And I say the thing that I *know* will push him over the edge.

"If you walk away from this now," I whisper, "you'll never stop wondering."

His breath catches.

And in that moment, I know.

He won't walk away.

Not this time.

Beau leans against the porch railing, exhaling deeply.

"Okay," he says, his voice low, steady. "We do this. But on my terms."

I nod. "That's fair."

His eyes flick to mine. "That means you don't go near Jesse without me."

I hesitate but only for a second. "Okay."

He studies me. "Promise me, Daisy."

I press my lips together, my stomach twisting. I *hate* making promises I don't know if I can keep.

But I know he needs to hear it.

I give him *something close enough to the truth.*

"I won't let Jesse pull me into something I can't handle."

Beau doesn't look convinced.

But for now, it's enough.

And as we stand there, the night stretching around us, the weight of what's coming settles between us.

We don't know what Jesse really wants.

We don't know what he'll say.

We don't know if the past we're chasing is better left buried.

But one thing is clear.

Whatever happens next, we're in it together.

Chapter 8
The Second Meeting

I should feel better.

Beau let me in.

For the first time since Jesse showed up, he told me the truth—not the carefully controlled version, not the version where he tries to carry it all on his own, but the *real* one.

And yet I don't feel better, I feel worse.

Because now that I *know*, I can't stop *thinking*.

I can't stop picturing Aaron, standing at some crossroads, believing he had a way out and believing Beau would be there to help him.

I can't stop imagining the moment Jesse turned up instead.

The moment it all went wrong.

And I *definitely* can't stop replaying the way Jesse said, *you can only bury the past for so long, Montgomery.*

Like he knew this was coming.

Like he *planned* for it.

I grip my coffee mug tighter, the ceramic warm in my hands as I sit at my kitchen table, staring out the window at the early morning mist rolling through the trees.

I haven't slept.

Not really.

Beau left hours ago, needing space to clear his head, needing *time* before we go through with whatever this is.

I told him I understood.

And I do.

But the longer I sit here, the worse it gets.

Because I *need answers*.

And I need them *now*.

By the time the clock hits nine, I've already made up my mind.

I grab my keys.

I know what I promised Beau.

I know what he asked of me.

But *I can't sit here and do nothing*.

I *need* to talk to Jesse.

Alone.

Finding Jesse isn't hard.

I don't know how I *knew*, but the second I step into town, I spotted him at the edge of the square, leaning against the side of his car like he has nowhere else to be.

Like he was *waiting*.

The sight of him sends a shiver up my spine.

But I won't stop moving.

I walk straight toward him, my boots clicking against the pavement.

He lifts his gaze as I approach, amusement flickering across his face.

"Well, well." His lips curve into something lazy. "Didn't expect you to be the one to come find me."

I stop a few feet away, arms crossed. "Yeah? Well, maybe you shouldn't be so predictable."

Jesse chuckles. "Fair enough."

I don't return the smile.

I don't *blink*.

Because I know what this is—what he *wants* this to be.

A game.

And I refuse to let him win.

"You said Beau owes you something," I say, my voice sharper than I intended. "What did you mean?"

Jesse tilts his head. "Did he send you?"

"No."

He studies me. "Does he know you're here?"

I hesitate.

That's all the answer he needs.

His grin widens. "Trouble in paradise?"

My patience snaps. "Tell me what happened that night."

Jesse exhales dramatically. "So *demanding*."

I step closer. "Don't—"

"Careful, Daisy."

Something shifts in his tone, something *calculated*.

"Beau doesn't like when people dig too deep into the past," he murmurs, watching me carefully. "You sure you want to be the one to do it?"

My breath hitches.

Because that's *exactly* what I'm afraid of.

That if I keep pushing, if I keep asking, if I don't let this go, Beau will break.

Or worse— We will.

I swallow. "I don't need you to tell me what Beau wants. I need you to tell me what *you* want."

Jesse leans in slightly, his voice lowering.

"I want him to *remember*."

A chill runs down my spine.

"Remember *what*?" I whisper.

Jesse's smirk fades. "What really happened that night."

My stomach clenches.

"He *knows* what happened," I snap.

Jesse's gaze darkens. "Does he?"

I take a step back, my mind racing.

"I—"

"Careful, Daisy," Jesse says again, but this time, it's not teasing.

This time, it's a *warning*.

Because suddenly, I know.

I know Jesse isn't just here for revenge.

He's here because there's something Beau *doesn't remember*.

And whatever it is, I think it threatens to change everything.

I barely register walking away from Jesse.

My thoughts are spiraling, my pulse pounding as I push through town, past the bakery, past the square, past everything.

I need to *think*.

I need to *breathe*.

I need—

"Daisy."

I jolt, whipping around.

Beau.

He's standing in front of my flower shop, brows drawn tight, his hands shoved deep in his pockets.

His expression? well it's not good.

"Where the hell were you?"

My stomach just drops.

I *hesitate*—too long, just long enough for Beau to *see* it.

His jaw clenches. "Daisy."

I lick my lips, my pulse hammering. "I—"

"Tell me you didn't go see him."

I don't answer though and that's the problem.

Beau exhales sharply, dragging a hand through his hair before taking a step forward, his voice low and tight.

"I asked you to stay away from him." His eyes never leaving mine.

I flinch. "Beau—"

"You *promised* me."

Guilt stabs deep into my ribs.

I *did*.

But—

"You weren't going to do anything!" I snap, my voice cracking. "You were just going to *wait* until Jesse decided to show his hand, and I—I *couldn't*."

Beau's face is unreadable.

"And what did he say?" His voice is eerily calm.

I hesitate, contemplating how I should address this situation.

Beau's lips press into a thin line. "Daisy."

I exhale, my breath shaky. "He said you don't remember something."

Beau *freezes* but only for a second, just long enough to confirm it.

"Beau," I whisper, my chest aching. "Is that true?"

I'm met with a long, heavy pause.

Then Beau mumbles,

"I remember *enough*."

The words feel like a knife to the gut.

I shake my head, my hands trembling. "No. No, you don't get to *do that*—you don't get to stand there and tell me I'm supposed to trust you when you *won't even trust yourself*."

Beau exhales sharply, his body tense. "Daisy—"

"Tell me what you're so afraid to remember!" I demand.

The silence is thick and suffocating.

"You don't want to know." Beau states.

The words send a *shockwave* through me.

Because it's not a *threat*.

It's a *warning*.

A deep, *aching* warning from a man who has spent *years* keeping something buried.

And suddenly—

I don't know if I want to dig it up.

Because maybe, just *maybe*—

Some truths should stay buried.

I don't sleep. I barely breathe. I spend the entire night pacing my living room, my mind racing and my heart pounding. Because now I know.

Jesse isn't lying. There is something Beau doesn't remember—or something he refuses to remember.

And whatever it is, it's bad enough that he would rather risk losing me than face it.

The thought coils around me like a vice. I replay every moment, every conversation, every look I thought I understood. My chest tightens as I start to wonder if the man I trusted, the man I believed in, has been hiding a truth dark enough to destroy everything.

I stop pacing. My pulse roars in my ears.

My vision blurs. For the first time, I don't know who I can believe. The world tilts, and the ground beneath me feels like it's cracking apart. And that terrifies me.

Chapter 9
The Breaking Point

I can feel myself unraveling, it's not just doubt anymore.

It's something much *worse*; it's fear.

A deep, gnawing fear that has sunk its claws into my chest and won't let go.

I *should* trust Beau. I do trust Beau, don't I?

I rake my fingers through my hair, pacing the length of my living room, the floor creaking beneath my frantic steps.

The shadows outside have stretched long and thin, the soft golden glow of the streetlights casting strange patterns across the walls. The clock on my mantle ticks—steady, relentless, mocking.

It's late. Way too late and I know I should stop.

What I should do is go to bed. I should turn off my mind. I should wait for morning, wait for Beau, wait for—for what?

More silence? More half-truths? More carefully controlled answers that don't tell me a damn thing?

I shake my head, frustration clawing at my chest.

I can't.

I *won't.*

Because something is *wrong*, and I feel it in my *bones.*

Jesse *knew* what he was doing when he said Beau doesn't remember.

And Beau he flinched; not in denial and not in anger but in fear.

And if *Beau Montgomery*—the man who has survived more than most, who has held himself together with iron will and quiet strength—*is afraid to remember?*

Then *maybe I should be afraid, too.*

The thought makes me shudder.

But it doesn't stop me.

Because the fear is nothing compared to the need to know.

I whirl around, grabbing my phone from the table, my fingers shaking as I type out a message.

Daisy: *Meet me now.*

The reply is instant.

Jesse: *Knew you'd come around.*

The night air is sharp, cold, wrapping around me as I step out into the quiet streets of Willow Creek.

Most of the town is asleep.

Lights flicker in a few second-story apartments above Main Street, the warm glow of bedside lamps illuminating silhouettes against the windows.

But down here?

Down here, it feels like the world is *holding its breath*.

Like it's *waiting* for me to make a mistake.

I walk faster.

Jesse told me where to meet him—*the old train station on the outskirts of town.*

It hasn't been in use for years. The tracks are rusted; the wooden platform cracked with time. A single streetlight flickers weakly at the edge of the lot, casting long, broken shadows across the gravel.

It's *exactly* the kind of place someone meets when they don't want to be seen.

And I should be nervous.

I *am* nervous.

But the need for answers is louder.

Jesse is already there when I arrive, leaning against a metal railing, cigarette dangling between his fingers.

He smirks when he sees me.

"Knew you wouldn't be able to let it go," he murmurs, exhaling smoke into the night air.

I ignore the way his gaze drags over me, the way he *acts* like he knows me, like he's already won.

"Tell me," I say, crossing my arms. "Tell me what Beau doesn't remember."

Jesse tilts his head, tapping ash onto the ground.

"You *sure* you wanna know?"

A chill runs down my spine.

Because the way he says it—

It's not a *question*.

It's a *dare*.

And suddenly, I wonder if I should run.

If I should turn around, go home, wait for Beau, let him tell me in his own time, his own way—

But it's *too late*.

Because Jesse's already speaking.

And the words that come next?

They change *everything*.

"Aaron was scared that night."

I freeze trying to take in the words I am hearing.

Jesse flicks his cigarette onto the ground, crushing it beneath his boot.

"He wasn't just leaving," he continues, his voice dropping lower. "He was running."

My heart stutters. "Running *from what?*"

Jesse smirks, but there's something *darker* behind it now.

"From *Beau*."

The words slam into me like a punch to the gut.

I shake my head. "That's not—"

"Oh, it's true." Jesse steps closer, his voice a slow, deliberate drawl. "Aaron told me himself. He said he *had to leave*, because if he didn't—"

He pauses but only for a beat, for a single breath

Then he continues on,

"Beau was going to *kill* him."

It feels like the world *tilts*.

I stumble back a step, my ears ringing, my chest *burning*.

"No." My voice is barely a whisper. "That's *not*—"

Jesse shrugs. "Believe what you want. But that's the truth, sweetheart."

My hands are shaking. My pulse is *roaring*.

Beau wouldn't—

He *wouldn't*.

But Jesse's eyes they're too damn sure, what reason would he have to lie about this.

It's as if the world has stolen the air from my lungs, leaving me gasping in silence. I can't—believe him or this.

"You okay there, Daisy?" Jesse murmurs, voice laced with amusement.

I *snap* back to reality.

"*Why* would Aaron think that?" I demand, my voice raw, desperate.

Jesse arches a brow. "You already know the answer."

My stomach twists.

Beau doesn't remember something, but whatever it is it's something huge.

Something that made Aaron think he was in danger.

Something—Jesse knows more then he's telling me.

I grab his shirt, shoving him back against the railing.

"Tell me," I hiss. "Tell me what you're not saying."

Jesse grins, his breath warm against my cheek.

"Make Beau remember."

I push away from him, my hands trembling, my thoughts *spiraling*.

I keep telling myself I can't, that I don't believe him, because none of this makes sense. This isn't real, it can't be real, I don't know what to believe but Beau doesn't remember; so what Jesse is saying could be true, my brain feels like its battling its own inner monologue. As Jesse just watches me.

Like he's *waiting*.

Like he *knows* what's about to happen next.

And maybe—just maybe he does.

I don't remember leaving.

I don't remember walking back through town, past the empty streets, past the buildings that suddenly feel too small, too wrong.

I only remember the panic.

I don't realize I'm crying until I'm gripping my kitchen counter, my breath coming in sharp, *ragged* gasps.

Aaron thought Beau was going to kill him. Beau doesn't remember. Beau is hiding something from himself, something dark and terrifying that even he can't face. And Jesse; Jesse knows exactly what it is.

I press my hands to my face, a sob tearing out of my chest, because I love Beau. I love him more than anything. But the thought claws at me: what if I've spent this entire time loving a man who is capable of something I can't even begin to imagine? My hands shake, my mind spins, and I can't think. I can't breathe. I can't—

Then a loud bang echoes through the night, cutting through the fear and throwing everything into sharp, dangerous focus.

I *jolt*, my breath hitching, my pulse *spiking*.

A second later, I hear it.

My front door—

Someone is pounding on my front door.

I freeze, my stomach twisting into a tight, painful knot.

And then—

"Daisy!"

My entire body locks up.

Because I know that voice.

I know that voice *better than my own heartbeat*.

It's *Beau*.

And suddenly—

I don't know if I want to let him in.

Chapter 10
The Final Confrontation

BANG. BANG. BANG.

"Daisy, open the door!"

Beau's voice cuts through the night, rough and desperate, sending a shockwave through me.

I *freeze*.

My pulse is thundering, my breath ragged as I grip the edge of my kitchen counter, trying to anchor myself.

But I can't, my world has just shifted.

Because Jesse's words are still ringing in my head, twisting around my thoughts, warping everything I thought I knew.

"Aaron was running."

"Not from Jesse. From Beau."

"Beau was going to kill him."

No, no it can't be true. Trying to shake these thoughts from my brain.

But what if it is? Is the pestering question that keeps lingering behind all these thoughts.

That thought sends a violent shudder through me, my stomach twisting.

Another bang on the door.

"*Daisy!*"

I *should* answer him, I should let him in but the fear is too thick, too real.

Because I don't know what's standing on the other side of that door anymore.

I don't know who Beau *really* is and maybe I never truly did.

Not when there's an entire piece of that night missing.

And if he doesn't remember—

What happens when he *does*?

I take a shaky breath, forcing my feet to move, dragging with each step, crossing the room until I'm standing in front of the door.

My fingers brush the handle—And I stop.

Just listening I can hear Beau breathing hard on the other side. I can almost feel each haggard breath he takes.

The barely contained storm in his voice when he speaks again.

"Daisy, *please.*" His voice cracks with desperation.

I swallow, pressing my forehead against the cool wood, my chest *aching*.

"I—" My voice *breaks*. "I don't know if I can."

The silence held for a breath, and then it broke with a single stunned word.

"...What?"

A sharp exhale, like I just hit him square in the ribs.

I squeeze my eyes shut. "I don't know if I can open the door, Beau."

There's a beat, just long enough to feel the weight of the silence then his voice drops low and dangerous. "What did he tell you?"

I flinch. "Beau—"

"No." His tone sharpens, slicing through my hesitation like a blade. "You went to see him, didn't you?"

I don't answer because I don't need too, he already knows.

A *harsh* sound leaves him; something caught between a curse and a ragged breath.

"I asked you... no *I begged you* to stay away from him."

Something inside me finally snaps, like the thin thread I've been holding onto finally gives way.

"And you think I could after the way you looked at me?" My voice cracks, raw and trembling. "Beau, you *flinched*. You acted like there was something to be afraid of, and I—" My breath hitches. "I had to know."

The following silence is heavy, too thick, too telling. I still can't bring myself to open the door.

"What did he say?" Beau's voice is *deadly quiet*.

I shake my head, my hands shaking. "I don't know if I believe him."

A *sharp* laugh from the other side. "That's not what I asked."

My throat tightens.

"He said Aaron was running."

A slow exhale. "Daisy—"

"He said it wasn't from him."

I can almost hear his breathing stilling from behind the door. I know before I even say it—

"He said it was from *you.*"

For a moment, I think I've broken something in him. The silence that follows isn't just the absence of sound; it feels like a void stretching between us, deep and endless, as if something fragile has finally snapped.

When Beau speaks at last, his voice is almost unrecognizable; it's low and hoarse, edged with something dangerous. "You think I hurt him?"

A shudder runs through me. "I don't—"

"You think I would have killed him?"

My breath catches as panic surges through me. "Beau, please—"

His laugh cuts through the air, hollow and sharp. "Jesus Christ."

I flinch, because what I hear in his voice isn't anger. It's something far worse. It's pain.

He drags in a shaky breath, but this time it sounds sharper, less restrained, as though he's unraveling with every second that passes. "Open the door, Daisy."

I tell myself I can't, that I shouldn't, but I know I have to. My hand trembles as I reach for the handle, and when I unlock it the door swings wide, revealing him; not just Beau Montgomery, but a version of him that looks as though he is carrying the weight of every ghost he has ever tried to bury. His eyes meet mine, and for the first time I see him looking at me as if I have just become one of them.

Beau steps inside, his movements slow and deliberate like he's trying to keep himself together.

The door clicks shut behind him and I feel like I can barely breathe.

I see his jaw is *clenched*, his hands flexing at his sides like he doesn't trust himself to move.

Then he lifts his gaze to mine, And I swear my heart stops, because I can see it. The truth or at least the weight of it.

My voice shakes. "Beau—"

"I don't remember what happened after Aaron left Jesse's that night."

The confession hits *like a gunshot*.

Because that's what Jesse said, isn't it?

"Make Beau remember."

A slow, sickening chill rolls through me.

My lips part, but no sound comes out.

Because for the first time Beau looks afraid of himself. He swallows hard, his voice barely above a whisper.

"I *woke up* covered in blood, Daisy."

A sharp, violent breath wrenches from my chest.

"No, no, no." Beau shakes his head, his hands dragging through his hair as his breath comes faster, unraveling him. "I don't know how I got there. I don't know what I did. I don't—" He cuts himself off, his body locking as though the words are too heavy. "Aaron was gone, and I was just... there."

My knees nearly give way, and I press a hand to the wall to steady myself. "Beau—"

"I don't know if I hurt him."

The admission guts me. Beau has never lied to me, not about this, and if he's saying it now, then he truly doesn't know what happened.

Panic claws at my chest as he exhales, dragging a hand down his face. "I wanted to kill Jesse," he says hoarsely. "But Aaron? I loved my brother."

I press a shaking hand to my mouth as his voice cracks. "But what if Jesse was right? What if Aaron was running from me?"

He looks at me like I'm his last hope, like I'm the only thing keeping him from breaking. I want to reach for him, but doubt holds me back. If Beau doesn't know what he did that night, how am I supposed to?

The thought splinters something inside me, and before I realize it, I step back. His expression shatters, as if I've just confirmed his greatest fear. And in that moment, I understand that this isn't just breaking us. It might destroy us.

Something inside Beau snaps. His chest rises and falls in sharp, jagged breaths, his hands curling into fists as if he is trying to hold himself together but already knows he is losing the battle. He drags a hand across his face and mutters, "Why me?!"

I take another step back, my voice shaking. "Beau, I—"

"No." His voice is raw, trembling, barely holding together. "You think I—" He cuts himself off, shaking his head violently, as if the words are too poisonous to let out, as if just saying them would make him sick.

Tears blur my vision as I wipe at my face, my hands trembling. "I don't know, okay? I don't know what to think, and that's the problem."

"That's the problem?" His voice rises, frustration spilling over. "The problem isn't Jesse coming back to mess with my head? The problem isn't that he is trying to get inside yours? The problem is me?"

I don't answer. I can't. Because I don't know. I don't know what's worse: the fact that I asked the question at all, or the fact that Beau doesn't seem sure of the answer himself.

His breath shudders as he grips the back of his neck, his whole-body tense and shaking. Then, quietly but firmly, he says, "I can't do this right now."

The words tear through me. I stiffen. "What?"

He turns away, dragging his hands through his hair, his shoulders tight with something I cannot reach. "I can't do this. Not right now. Not when—" He cuts himself off again, leaving the rest unsaid.

I stare at him, and suddenly I understand. He is leaving. Again.

A sob burns in my throat as I whisper, "Beau—"

"I can't."

And then he is gone, walking out the door before I can stop him.

Just like that, I am alone. And for the first time in my life, I wonder if I have lost him for good.

Chapter 11
Aftershocks

I don't move; I don't even breathe. I just stand there.

Frozen in the middle of my living room, staring at the door that Beau just walked out of.

My pulse is a frantic drumbeat in my ears, drowning out everything else.

The house is too quiet. The silence isn't peaceful; it lingers like a weight, stretching into every corner until it feels unbearable.

The air is heavy, thick enough to press against my chest, as if it's trying to squeeze out the words that never left my mouth. Words I should have said. Words I should have said sooner.

I should have stopped him. I should have fought harder. I should have done anything to keep him here.

But I didn't.

And now, I don't know if I'll get another chance.

Because for the first time since I met him, Beau Montgomery walked away from me.

And I don't know if he's coming back.

I don't know how long I stand there.

Minutes. Hours. A lifetime.

Time stretches and folds in on itself, and all I can do is replay the moment over and over again in my head.

I can still see the way his jaw tightened, the way his voice broke, and the way he looked at me as though I was the only thing holding him together—only to let go. A sob claws its way up my throat, sharp and desperate, but I force it back down. I can't break. Not yet.

I make myself move, needing to do something, anything, before the weight of it crushes me. I sink onto the couch, pulling my knees to my chest and wrapping my arms around them as though I can hold myself together that way. My phone is already in my hand before I realize it, my thumb hovering over Beau's name. I could call him. I could fix this. But the thought twists inside me, because what if I can't? What if I've already lost him?

I press the heels of my hands against my eyes, dragging in shallow breaths and forcing the rising panic back down where it belongs. Just breathe. Just think. Just do something.

The front door slams open, jolting me upright, my breath catching painfully in my throat. For a fleeting, foolish second, I think it's Beau. But it isn't.

It's Maggie.

The moment she sees me; her entire face softens. "Oh, Daisy..."

And that's all it takes. I break.

One second, I'm holding it in—

The next, I'm full-on sobbing into Maggie's shoulder, my fingers clutching at her like she's the only thing keeping me from *falling apart completely.*

"I don't— I don't know what just happened," I gasp, my voice raw and ragged. "He just—he *left*."

Maggie tightens her arms around me. "I know, honey."

I shake my head frantically. "No, you *don't*. You don't know what Jesse said, or what Beau admitted, or—"

Maggie pulls back, gripping my shoulders. "Then tell me."

So, I do and I tell her everything from when I went to see Jesse to how he told me that Aaron was afraid of Beau that night.

I tell her *every detail on how Beau doesn't remember and maybe just for one horrible second I wondered if it was true.*

Maggie listens, her expression shifting from concern to frustration to something *almost* like fear.

When I finally finish, my hands are shaking, my throat raw.

She exhales, dragging a hand through her curls. "Jesus, Daisy."

I sniffle. "What if I was wrong about him?"

Maggie's expression *hardens*. "You don't really believe that."

I open my mouth just as fast as I close it because honestly, I just don't know what I believe anymore.

My head and my heart are at war, and I'm stuck in the middle, drowning.

Maggie studies me for a long moment, her eyes searching mine as if testing whether I'm ready. The silence lingers, heavy, until she finally asks, soft but steady.

"Do you want the truth?"

I nod once slow, even though I'm not so sure I do.

She exhales. "You *did* screw up by going to Jesse."

Pain lances through me. "I—"

"But," she cuts in, "Beau *also* screwed up by shutting you out."

I blink. "So we both—"

"Yeah." She gives me a pointed look. "You both need to get your shit together."

I let out a watery laugh. "Great. Any advice on *how*?"

Maggie sighs. "That depends."

I frown. "On what?"

She levels me with a serious look.

"On whether you *actually* believe Beau could've hurt Aaron."

A lump lodges itself in my throat.

Because that's the *real* question, isn't it?

That's what's been eating me alive all night.

And the truth is—

"No." My voice is barely above a whisper. "I don't believe he could have done that."

Maggie's face softens. "Then tell him that."

I swallow hard. "What if it's too late?"

Maggie arches a brow. "Do you *really* think Beau is the kind of guy to just walk away from you forever?"

I want to say no. I need to say no.

The word is right there, caught at the back of my throat, begging to be spoken.

But then I remember the way he looked at me before he left. Like I wasn't just someone, but as if I was everything, the one thing he couldn't handle losing.

I don't know what I feel, or what I'm supposed to feel and that terrifies me more than I can admit.

The next morning, I wake up feeling like I barely slept, because in reality I didn't.

I tossed and turned all night, my thoughts running in circles, my chest *aching* from the weight of it all.

Beau still hasn't called, not even so much as a text message.

And every hour that passes without him feels like another brick pressing down on my ribs.

Maggie made me promise to give him space, to let him come to me.

The lingering fear that keeps nagging on me is what if he doesn't?

Suddenly, a knock at the door jolts me upright and my heart lurches.

I scramble out of bed, barely managing to tug on a sweater before yanking the door open.

And there he is, standing on my porch looking like hell is Beau.

I can't help but stare his eyes are bloodshot, his jaw unshaven, his whole-body *tense*.

It's as if he spent the entire night *thinking*, almost like he's breaking just as much as I am.

I grip the doorframe to steady myself.

"Hi," I breathe.

Beau exhales. "Hey."

Silence stretches between us, thick and heavy.

I don't know what to say.

I don't know *how* to fix this.

"I need to tell you everything," he says quietly.

My breath catches. "Beau—"

"I don't remember that night," he admits, his voice *rough*. "But I know Jesse isn't telling the whole truth. And I know—"

He hesitates, his throat working as his Adam's apple bobs up and down.

"I know I can't lose you over this."

My chest *tightens*.

Beau takes a slow, shaking breath, his gaze locked onto mine.

"If you still believe in me," he murmurs, "then help me figure out what really happened."

The air *crackles* between us.

In this moment, this choice is the one that will decide every-thing.

I keep telling myself that I know there's still so much left un-spoken and so much left undone, but to walk away now? And give up isn't an option for me or him.

I reach for his hand, gripping it tightly.

"I believe in you," I whisper.

Beau exhales sharply, like those words are the only thing holding him together.

"Then let's find out the truth."

And just like that— we aren't falling apart anymore, were fight-ing this together.

Chapter 12

The Hunt for the Truth

I don't let go of Beau's hand.

Not when the wind picks up, sending the scent of damp earth and autumn leaves swirling around us. Not when the weight of everything still left unsaid presses against my ribs, making it harder to breathe. Not even when I feel the tension in his fingers; the way his grip tightens, like he's still waiting for me to change my mind.

Because I *won't*. Not now and not when I finally see him again.

Not the version of Beau who walked away last night, his jaw tight, his shoulders set like a man ready to disappear.

This Beau? The one standing in front of me, eyes heavy with exhaustion but filled with something new, something sharp with determination is the man I fell in love with.

The man I believe in.

And I need him to know that.

I squeeze his hand. "Where do we start?"

Beau exhales, dragging his free hand through his hair. "Jesse's been playing mind games since the second he came back. If we want to figure out what really happened that night..." His jaw tightens. "We start with him."

A shiver runs down my spine.

Jesse.

The one who lit the match and set this fire.

The one who whispered his poison in my ear and watched me *break* from it.

I nod, swallowing past the lump in my throat. "Then let's go."

The drive to Jesse's place is too quiet.

Beau grips the wheel, his knuckles white, his jaw set.

I steal a glance at him, at the way his chest rises and falls a little too fast, at the way his fingers flex like he's trying to keep himself from gripping something harder like he wants to hit something.

Or *someone*.

I reach over, placing my hand on his thigh, a silent anchor.

Beau exhales slowly, like I just pulled him back from the edge.

"I hate this," he mutters.

I nod. "I know."

His throat bobs. "I hate that you even had to *consider* the possibility..." He shakes his head, gripping the wheel tighter. "That I could've done something like that."

Guilt crashes over me like a wave.

"Beau—"

"No," he cuts in, his voice rough. "I get why you did. I get why you went to him, why you had to hear it for yourself. But, Daisy..." He glances at me, his eyes dark and *serious*. "If you ever need answers again, come to *me* first."

A knot forms in my stomach but he's right I should have.

I should have *trusted* that he would tell me the truth.

I nod, my fingers tightening against his leg. "I will."

The tension between us softens, just a little.

But as we pull up to Jesse's place it's a run-down bar on the outskirts of town that he calls "home" , something thick and electric settles in the air again.

Because this?

This is where everything changes.

Jesse is waiting for us.

He leans against the hood of his car, a cigarette dangling from his fingers, his smirk lazy and expectant. Like he *knew* we'd come.

Like he's been *waiting* for it.

Beau kills the engine. His body is coiled so tight I can feel the tension radiating off of him.

I touch his arm. "Let me lead."

Beau lets out a sharp breath but nods.

I climb out first, stepping forward, my pulse hammering in my ears.

Jesse exhales a long stream of smoke, watching me with something too amused in his eyes.

"Well, well," he drawls. "Look who's finally ready for the truth."

I stop a few feet from him, forcing my voice to stay steady. "I want everything you didn't say last time."

Jesse chuckles. "Sweetheart, I already gave you the best parts."

A muscle jumps in Beau's jaw as he steps up beside me. "Then give us the rest."

Jesse's smirk widens. "Feisty."

Beau *steps forward.*

I grab his arm before he can do something we'll both regret.

Jesse just watches, exhaling another lazy drag of his cigarette. "Relax, Montgomery. You're wound up so tight you're about to snap."

Beau doesn't respond.

But I *see* it in the way his muscles coil, the way his breathing hitches.

Jesse notices, too.

He's thriving off of it and he loves it.

I grit my teeth. "What aren't you telling us?"

Jesse taps ash onto the ground, tilting his head like he's considering his options. "Aaron ran that night. That part wasn't a lie."

My chest tightens. "Because he was afraid?"

Jesse hums. "Because he *thought* he had a reason to be."

Beau stiffens. "Thought?"

Jesse flicks his cigarette to the ground, grinding it under his boot. "Tell me something, Montgomery—when was the last time you *really* tried to remember that night?"

Beau's jaw clenches. "I don't remember *because I was drunk*."

Jesse smiles, slow and smug. "Or because you don't *want* to."

The air *crackles* and in an instant Beau is lunging.

I barely manage to hold him back as Jesse laughs, his hands raised in mock surrender.

"Easy, cowboy. You want answers? You should be talking to *someone else*."

My stomach plummets at his words, a sickening weight settling low as dread coils through me. Someone else?

Jesse takes a deliberate step back, his grin stretching wider, taunting, as though he knows exactly how deep the knife is cutting. "Your old man, for starters."

The chill that sweeps through me is instant, turning my blood to ice.

Beside me, Beau doesn't move. He goes still unnervingly, terrifyingly still the kind of stillness that feels more dangerous than rage.

Jesse leans in, voice lower now. "You ever wonder why your *dad* kept his mouth shut all these years?"

Something *snaps* inside Beau.

He wrenches free of my grip, his fist *connecting* with Jesse's jaw in a sharp, brutal crack.

Jesse stumbles back, laughing as he wipes blood from his mouth.

"Oh, Montgomery," he taunts, his voice *dangerously amused*. "You *really* don't want to know, do you?"

Beau's breath is ragged, his fists still clenched.

I grab his arm again, my voice frantic. "Beau—*stop*."

He doesn't move.

He just stares at Jesse, his chest rising and falling too fast.

I look at Jesse, my heart hammering.

"Why would his dad know something?"

Jesse licks his lip, tasting the blood.

He grins like he's enjoying this and I hate it.

"Because, sweetheart..." He shakes his head. "Your boyfriend wasn't the only one who blacked out that night."

The ground shifts beneath me, tilting in a way that makes it hard to breathe. Beside me, Beau stiffens, every muscle locked tight.

And in that moment, we both understand.

Something we should have seen all along.

This was never just about Beau.

It was about the Montgomery family. About the secrets buried so deep they were never meant to surface.

And the one person who might finally hold the answers we've been searching for?

Beau's father.

We don't speak on the drive back.

Beau's grip on the wheel is tight, his knuckles white, his jaw locked.

I can feel the storm building inside him; the questions he can't voice, the rage simmering beneath the surface, and the fear he can't quite hide.

I reach for him, letting my fingers brush against his. He flinches at the contact, but then his hand closes over mine, tight and desperate, as if letting go would mean losing everything.

"Beau," I whisper.

His throat works as he swallows hard, his voice rough when it finally breaks the silence. "I have to talk to him."

I nod, my own heart hammering. "Then we go first thing in the morning."

Beau exhales slowly.

And in the silence that follows, I realize something.

We aren't just looking for answers anymore.

We're about to unearth something far worse.

And I don't know if we're ready for it.

Chapter 13
Digging Up the Past

The night is long Beau and I barely get any sleep.

I know because every time I drift into some fragile, restless dream, I wake up to the sound of him shifting beside me. The rustle of sheets, the deep, uneven breaths, the unbearable tension still radiating from his body.

It's not even about Jesse anymore.

It's about his father.

The man who had spent years keeping secrets.

The man who had never spoken about the night Aaron died.

And the man who, *if Jesse was telling the truth*, had *blacked out the same night Beau did.*

The thought makes my stomach turn.

Because whatever this is, isn't just about finding answers it's about who we can even trust anymore.

I roll over in bed, facing Beau. His eyes are open, staring at the ceiling, his jaw tight.

I reach for his hand, brushing my fingers over his knuckles. "Beau?"

His throat bobs. "Yeah?"

"Are you okay?"

His silence is deafening and after a long moment he replies,

"I don't know."

I squeeze his hand. "Then let's figure it out together."

Morning comes *too fast*.

It's cold and misty. The kind of early autumn day where the sky can't decide if it wants to rain or not.

We drive in silence.

Beau's hands are locked around the steering wheel like it's the only thing tethering him to reality. His jaw is clenched so tight I can see the tension in his neck.

I want to say something, to tell him that we'll get through this. That no matter what we find out, I'm here but I know better.

Right now, he's barely holding himself together.

So, I let the silence sit between us, thick and heavy, until we finally pull up to the one place Beau never wants to go.

The Montgomery Ranch.

Beau cuts the engine, but he doesn't move.

He just stares at the house.

I watch him, waiting, my heart hammering.

"Last time I was here," he murmurs, "he told me to stop asking questions."

I swallow hard. "Then maybe it's time he starts answering them."

Beau exhales slowly, rubbing a hand over his face.

Then he nods and we make our way out.

The house is silent, so quiet it almost hums in my ears. Beau raps on the door once, the knock sharp and deliberate, but no answer comes. He tries again, louder this time, the sound echoing through the stillness. I'm just beginning to wonder if we'll have to track his father down somewhere else when the door finally creaks open.

James Montgomery stands in the doorway. Beau's father.

He looks older than I remember, though I can't decide if it's the way the morning light exaggerates the lines etched around his eyes, or the faint stubble shadowing his jaw, or simply the weariness that clings to him, most visible in the sharp, tired gaze that settles immediately on us. Maybe it's none of that at all. Maybe it's the way he seems to understand exactly why we've come before either of us has spoken a word.

Beau doesn't hesitate. "Why did you black out the night Aaron died?"

His father stiffens, every trace of composure turning to stone. The air changes instantly, heavy and suffocating, as though the oxygen itself has been stripped away.

James Montgomery looks at Beau. Then at me. And finally, back at his son.

"Come inside," he says.

The living room is cold, not the temperature. There's actually a fire crackling in the old stone fireplace but in the way it *feels* like it's frozen in time.

Like this house is still clinging to ghosts that refuse to leave.

James pours himself a drink of whiskey, straight but he doesn't offer us any.

Beau watches him like a predator sizing up a threat. "Talk...you know why I'm here"

James exhales through his nose, taking a slow sip. "You don't want to know."

Beau's voice sharpens. "*Yes, I do.*"

His father sets the glass down with a sharp *clink*.

"Alright, then," he mutters. "You want the truth? Here it is."

He leans forward, his gaze unflinching.

"I don't remember that night."

My stomach *drops* just as Beau stiffens.

"Bull that can't be true!" he snaps.

James doesn't flinch.

"I remember Aaron was here earlier that day," he continues, his voice unreadable. "I remember drinking. A lot. And then?" His jaw tightens. "Nothing. Just... *nothing*."

A chill runs down my spine.

Beau shakes his head, stepping forward. "You mean to tell me you and I both got so drunk that we blacked out the exact same night the same night my brother died and that's just supposed to be a damn coincidence?"

James doesn't move. "I don't know."

Beau lets out a *bitter laugh*, running a hand through his hair.

"You're lying."

James watches him carefully. "I'm not."

"Then what the hell happened?" Beau's voice cracks, frustration bleeding through. "Because Jesse seems to think you had a damn good reason to keep your mouth shut all these years."

Something flickers across James's expression, a shadow I can't quite name, here and gone before I can grasp it. And then his voice cuts through the silence. "You've been talking to Jesse?"

The shift is immediate. The exhaustion that clung to him, the almost passive irritation he carried a moment ago both vanish. What replaces them is something far more dangerous.

Beau doesn't flinch. He doesn't even blink. "Yeah. And he's telling me things that make a hell of a lot more sense than you do right now."

James rises abruptly, the motion so sudden and forceful that the whiskey glass tips over and crashes to the floor. The sound jolts through me, sharp enough to make me jump.

"You don't listen to Jesse," he snaps, his voice low. Warning. "You don't trust a damn word that comes out of his mouth."

Beau's entire body coils tight. "Why?"

James just shakes his head, gripping the edge of the table like he's holding himself back.

"You're in over your head, son."

Beau exhales sharply, stepping closer. "Then put me back on solid ground."

Silence stretches between them, heavy and unyielding. James studies his son without a word, while Beau holds his ground, refusing to move or look away.

At last, James exhales, the sound ragged as his hand drags across the rough line of his jaw. When he finally speaks, his words are so low, so quiet, I almost convince myself I imagined them. But I didn't.

And the moment they register, a chill races through me.

"I think I was drugged that night."

Beau goes still. So do I.

James keeps going, his voice *raw*.

"I don't drink like that," he mutters. "Not enough to *black out completely*." His hands flex at his sides. "But that night? I lost *hours*."

He looks up, his eyes haunted.

"And the only person I remember seeing, other than Aaron?"

He swallows hard.

"Was Jesse."

A sharp breath *punches* from my lungs.

Beau *rears back*, his face white as a sheet.

"Are you telling me Jesse drugged you?" His voice is barely a whisper.

James exhales sharply. "I'm telling you, whatever happened that night?"

He meets Beau's gaze.

It's the first time I've ever seen *actual fear* in his father's eyes.

"I think Jesse knows a hell of a lot more than he's saying."

The floor tilts beneath me.

Beau doesn't move.

And suddenly, we're not just looking for answers anymore.

We're hunting a man who has been playing with us *from the very beginning*.

Jesse lied and he knows and we're about to find out why.

Chapter 14
The Edge of the Truth

Beau doesn't move. I don't even think he's taken a breath.

I can *feel* the storm raging inside him—see the tension in his shoulders, the fire burning behind his eyes.

His father's words are still hanging in the air, thick and suffocating.

I think Jesse knows a hell of a lot more than he's saying and he's just been throwing us on a continuous loop.

That one sentence changes *everything*.

It's like a switch has been flipped.

We came here looking for answers, thinking James Montgomery was the last missing piece.

Now we know that Jesse isn't just stirring up trouble, he's been orchestrating something.

Something that's been hiding in the shadows for years.

And suddenly, the memory of his smug, taunting smirk as he wiped blood from his lip slams into my mind.

"Oh, Montgomery... You really don't want to know, do you?"

He wanted us to dig, to peel back the layers and uncover something buried beneath it all. But what was it he expected us to find and why would he want us to find it now? The questions pound through me with relentless force, my heart slamming against my ribs as though it's trying to break free. I take a shaky breath, forcing myself to focus. "James..." My voice is softer now, careful. "Why do you think Jesse would drug you?"

His father exhales, rubbing a hand down his face. "I don't know." His voice is thick with frustration. "I've been asking myself the same damn question for years."

Beau scoffs, shaking his head. "And you never thought to tell me?"

James' gaze hardens. "Tell you *what*, Beau? That I woke up the next morning with no memory, no proof, nothing but a *feeling*?" He shakes his head. "You were already broken enough. I didn't see the point in adding more ghosts to your head."

Beau *laughs*—but there's no humor in it.

"So instead, you just let me walk around *hating myself*?" His voice is sharp, *wounded*. "You let me believe I might've been the one who hurt Aaron that night?"

James' expression flickers with something—regret, guilt, *shame*.

"I didn't know what else to do."

Beau takes a step forward, his fists clenching. "You could have told me the truth."

His father's jaw tightens. "And what if Jesse was lying?"

Silence hangs heavy between us, the weight of James's words landing like a punch to the gut. Because deep down, I know he's right and what if Jesse was only playing us? What if every step we've taken has been nothing more than chasing shadows, falling right into the trap he wanted? The thought coils cold in my chest.

But then my gut pushes back. No. Jesse knew we'd come looking. He wanted this. He set the trail for a reason.

Jesse knew exactly how to push Beau, how to plant the perfect seeds of doubt.

And now that we're finally piecing it together—

The question isn't *if* he's hiding something.

It's *what* he's waiting for us to find.

I swallow hard, my voice quiet but firm. "We need to go back to him."

Beau's head snaps toward me.

"Daisy—"

"No," I cut in, stepping closer. "This isn't just about the past anymore. It's about *right now*. Jesse didn't just keep quiet for all these years. He *baited* you into coming after him. And we need to figure out *why* before it's too late."

Beau clenches his jaw. "And if we don't like what we find?"

I take a deep breath.

"Then we find a way to stop it."

The air is heavy with tension as we pull up to Jesse's place. One thing I notice is that it's too quiet.

The kind of silence that warns you something is wrong before you even step inside.

Beau doesn't even bother knocking this time.

He throws the truck into park, slams the door shut, and storms straight for Jesse's front door.

I scramble to keep up. "Beau, wait—"

But it's too late. He bangs on the door once, twice, then shoves it open without waiting for an answer. The moment we step inside, the world seems to tilt beneath me.

The living room is a disaster. Furniture is overturned, glass litters the floor, and papers are strewn in every direction. It looks as though someone tore through the place in a hurry, searching for something or maybe trying to erase every trace of what had been here.

My stomach drops as the thought hits me. Someone was covering their tracks.

Beau is already moving, pushing through the chaos, his breath heavy as he calls out, "Jesse?"

There is no answer.

I follow behind him, scanning the wreckage. The couch cushions are slashed open, drawers pulled from the cabinets, liquor bottles shattered against the walls.

My eyes land on something, a piece of paper, half-crumpled and covered in smeared blood.

My breath catches, sharp and sudden. "Beau."

He turns, his expression dark and unreadable. I sink to my knees, snatching up the paper and smoothing it out with hands that won't stop shaking. It's a note, scrawled in messy, frantic handwriting, and it contains only four words: *"You're too late, Montgomery."*

The room seems to tilt, and my stomach drops as I stare at it. Beau grabs the note from my hands, his fingers tightening around the edges as his breathing becomes shallow and uneven. I can see it all there, written across his face the panic, the rage, the fear.

"We need to find him," I whisper.

Beau doesn't speak. He doesn't move. And then, after a long, trembling moment, he takes a slow, shaking breath and laughs—a hollow, dangerous sound that makes me stiffen.

"Beau—" I begin.

"He planned this," he says, his voice sharp, cutting through the air like a blade. "He knew we'd come back."

A cold shiver runs down my spine. "Then where is he now?"

Beau's jaw tightens, and in that instant, it hits us both at the same time. Jesse wasn't just running. He was leading us some-where.

His voice drops low, haunted, and almost quiet. "There's only one place left to go."

I swallow hard, already knowing where he means—the place we've been avoiding, the place where it all started, the place that has been waiting for us this entire time. Beau grips my hand tightly, and when he speaks again, his voice is deadly calm.

"The lake."

The drive is a blur, each mile slipping past in a haze of worry and anticipation. By the time we reach the lake, the sun is dipping low, casting an eerie golden light over the water that shimmers like liquid fire. And there, on the dock, a single figure waits.

Jesse. Alive. Unbothered. Smirking as though he knew we would come.

Beau is out of the truck before I can stop him, storming toward Jesse with murder in his eyes, every step radiating the fury he can barely contain. Jesse doesn't flinch. He doesn't move. He simply watches, that infuriating smirk never leaving his face.

"Montgomery," he drawls, the word dripping with mockery. "Took you long enough."

Beau stops just inches from him; fists clenched so tightly his knuckles whiten. "You're going to tell me everything," he growls, voice low and dangerous.

Jesse chuckles, the sound cold and calculated. "Oh, I will," he says, tilting his head, eyes glinting with something sharp and dangerous. "But first—"

He gestures toward the water. The lake. The same lake where Aaron died. The same lake where the truth has been buried for years.

Jesse smiles again, that impossible, infuriating smile. "I think it's time we dug up the past, don't you?"

My blood runs cold because I know; truly know that whatever comes next is going to change everything. Forever.

Book 4 to be released on December 21, 2025

Preview

Sneak Peek: Winter's Wish

Prepare yourself for the heartwarming conclusion of the Hearts in Bloom series with "Winter's Wish." As the snow blankets the charming town of Maplewood, hidden desires and unspoken dreams come to the surface. Clara Bridges invites you to a world where winter magic ignites hope, and love finds its way through the frost.

In "Winter's Wish," you'll journey alongside characters embarking on a path of self-discovery and genuine connection. Can the chill of winter reveal the warmth of true love? Immerse yourself in this captivating finale to see if wishes really do come true.

Stay Connected with Clara Bridges:

Follow Clara on Amazon to keep up with her latest works and special offers.
https://www.amazon.com/stores/Clara-Bridges/author/B0C HDV55TK

Connect with LPS Publishing House across all major platforms for the freshest updates on new releases and author events.

www.lpspublishing.com

@lps.publishing.house.llc – TikTok

https://www.facebook.com/profile.php?id=10009016787343
7 Facebook

Please enjoy:

Here is the Prologue to Winter's Wish

Prologue: *The Calm Before the Storm*

The first snowfall of the season comes quietly.

I watch from the window of my flower shop as delicate flakes drift down in lazy spirals, settling over Willow Creek like a fresh start. The streets are lined with twinkling holiday lights, their soft glow reflecting off the frosted sidewalks, and in the distance, I can hear the faint melody of Christmas carols playing from Main Street's speakers.

Everything looks *perfect*.

But I know better.

Because perfection is always fleeting.

I wrap my fingers around the warm mug of tea in my hands, letting the heat ground me. The scent of cinnamon and honey fills the air, blending with the ever-present fragrance of fresh flowers, but it does nothing to calm the unease curling in my stomach.

It's been weeks since everything with Jesse, since the night we stood in James Montgomery's house and uncovered the final piece of a mystery that had haunted Beau for years. Since the moment we realized just how deep the secrets ran.

Since the moment we learned that *the past was never really buried*.

I shiver, and not from the cold.

Beau doesn't talk about it much. Not outright. But I can see it in the way his shoulders tense when his phone buzzes unexpectedly. The way he keeps a wary eye on unfamiliar faces in town. The way he *still* hasn't told me exactly what his father said to him before we left that night.

He thinks he's protecting me.

And maybe he is.

But I also know that *secrets never stay hidden forever*.

A gust of wind rattles the shop door, and I snap out of my thoughts as the bell chimes, signaling someone's arrival.

Beau steps inside, shaking snow from his dark jacket, his cheeks flushed from the cold. His gaze lands on me instantly, his familiar blue-gray eyes softening as he takes me in.

"Hey, Daisy," he murmurs, crossing the space between us in a few long strides.

His voice is enough to make my stomach flip the way it always does. Even now, even after everything.

I set my mug down, letting him pull me into his warmth. His arms wrap securely around me, and for a moment, I close my eyes and breathe him in—fresh pine, leather, and *him*.

"Hey," I whisper back, resting my cheek against his chest. "How was your meeting with the mayor?"

"Long," he mutters, pressing a kiss to the top of my head. "They want the town square renovations done before the Winter Festival. Everyone's running on holiday cheer and blind optimism."

I smile against his jacket. "Sounds about right."

He exhales, his fingers tracing slow circles against my lower back. "What about you? Everything okay?"

I hesitate.

Because *yes*, everything *should* be okay.

I have Beau. My shop is thriving. The town is settling into the holiday season, filled with laughter and warmth.

And yet...

There's something lingering in the air. A feeling I can't quite name.

Like I'm waiting for the other shoe to drop.

I pull back slightly, forcing a smile as I look up at him. "Yeah. Everything's fine."

His brows knit together, like he doesn't quite believe me.

But before he can say anything, the shop door swings open again, and a blast of cold air rushes in—along with Maggie, her red curls wild beneath her knit hat.

"Alright, lovebirds, break it up," she teases, stomping snow from her boots. "We've got work to do if we're gonna make this Winter Festival the best one yet."

I glance at Beau, feeling his reluctant smile as he presses one last kiss to my forehead before letting me go.

Maggie grins at me. "Now *you* look like you've got something on your mind."

I shake my head, laughing softly. "Nothing important."

I don't tell her about the strange unease creeping beneath my skin.

I don't tell her about the way I sometimes catch Beau staring off into the distance, lost in thoughts he won't share.

I don't tell her that, despite the twinkling lights and the freshly fallen snow, something about this winter feels different.

Because I don't have proof.

Not yet.

But deep down, I know—

The past isn't done with us yet.

Also by

Clara Bridges, celebrated for her heartwarming romance novels, has captured the hearts of readers with her tales of love and redemption set in charming small-town settings. Here's a list of her enchanting works:

Wrong Flight to Love: A Small Town Sweet Romance
A delightful journey where mistaken paths lead to unexpected love.

A Rodeo Star's Homecoming: An Enemies to Lovers Clean Romance
An exciting tale of rivalry turned romance, set against the backdrop of rodeo life.

Above the Line: A Ski Lodge Enemies to Lovers Sweet Romance
Tension and affection collide in the scenic beauty of a snowy ski lodge.

Unwrapping the Past: A Christmas Tale of Redemption and Forgiveness
A heartwarming holiday story about healing old wounds and embracing new beginnings.

Whispers of Spring: A Small Town Love at First Sight Sweet Romance (Hearts in Bloom)

Love blossoms instantly in this tender tale of connection and renewal.

Summer's Embrace: A Small Town Second Chance Sweet Romance (Hearts in Bloom)

A story of rekindled romance in the warm embrace of summer.

www.ingramcontent.com/pod-product-compliance
Lightning Source LLC
Chambersburg PA
CBHW030148010826
48973CB00002B/781